sizzle in the sand

A Spicy Coffee Break Read

jessie cooke

redline publishing

Copyright © by Jessie Cooke

All rights reserved.

No part of this book may be reproduced in any form or by any electronic or mechanical means, including information storage and retrieval systems, without written permission from the author, except for the use of brief quotations in a book review.

a little note from me

I've always loved sharing stories with my friends—the juicy confessions and hilarious mishaps that spill out over coffee or cocktails, leaving us blushing, laughing, and completely losing track of time.

These quick, spicy reads channel that same buzz we feel when we finally stop caring who's watching and just let ourselves be.

I've set my naughty side free to bring you these mini coffee-break escapes—perfect for sneaking in whenever real life's a bit too much—just long enough to spark a flutter of excitement and a secret smile.

So go ahead, soak up the heat, savor the heart, and embrace that wink of truth woven into every steamy scene. I hope you love them as much as I love writing them.

Jess 😊

sizzle in the sand

. . .

"GIRL, you haven't gotten laid in what, eight months?" Sophia lounged across Phoebe's unmade bed, scrolling through her phone. "That beach getaway is exactly what your pussy needs."

Phoebe rolled her eyes but couldn't hide her smirk. "And you're sure you can't come? I got this amazing little cottage right on the sand."

"Some of us have to work, babe. Besides," Sophia sat up, her dark auburn curls bouncing, "you need this solo trip. Time to get your groove back."

An hour later, they were prowling through racks of swimwear at an upscale boutique downtown. Sophia kept pulling out increasingly skimpier options.

"Try this one." She thrust a barely-there white bikini at Phoebe. "Those perky tits of yours would look incredible."

In the dressing room, Phoebe studied her reflection. The tiny triangles of fabric just covered her nipples, the bottoms riding high on her hips to show off her tight ass. Her pale skin practically glowed against the white material.

"Holy fuck." Sophia whistled when Phoebe emerged. "If

you don't get railed wearing that, those beach boys must be blind."

They ended up with three bikinis...the white one, a royal blue that made Phoebe's eyes pop, and a black string number that left little to the imagination. Sophia insisted on some sheer cover-ups too, gossamer things that clung to every curve.

"Trust me." Sophia winked as they left the store, bags swinging. "By the end of this vacation, you'll have sand in places you didn't know existed and a smile that'll last for weeks."

Phoebe felt a familiar warmth building between her thighs just thinking about it. Maybe her friend was right...this trip was exactly what she needed.

―――

Back at their apartment, Phoebe stripped down to try on her purchases again, this time without the time pressure of the boutique changing room. Sophia sprawled on Phoebe's bed, critiquing each look.

"Mmm, the white one's still perfect," she purred as Phoebe turned. "Now try the black string one."

Phoebe slipped into the skimpiest bikini, adjusting the thin straps. "How's this looking?"

"Wait, what's that?" Sophia sat up, squinting. "Oh honey, your bush is literally escaping! Come here."

Phoebe looked down at her dark curls sneaking past the edges of the tiny bottoms. "Fuck, I didn't notice in the store."

"Why haven't you trimmed? That's practically a 70s porno bush down there!"

"Ughh, it's impossible," Phoebe groaned. "My hair's so coarse, it just turns into sharp stubble. Drives me crazy."

"Well, you can't go to the beach like that unless you're

trying to attract some granola dude with a VW van." Sophia hopped up. "Come on, bathroom. Now."

Minutes later, Phoebe was perched naked on the edge of the tub, legs spread as Sophia knelt between them with scissors and a razor.

"Jesus, it really is a jungle down here," Sophia muttered, carefully trimming the thick curls. Her warm breath tickled Phoebe's inner thighs.

"Mmmph." Phoebe bit her lip as Sophia's fingers brushed her sensitive flesh, positioning the hair for precise cuts. Her clit throbbed with each accidental touch.

"Stay still," Sophia commanded, working the razor in gentle strokes. "Almost done... there!"

Phoebe looked down at her newly groomed pussy, neat and tidy. Sophia's expert handiwork had left just enough to be sexy while keeping everything contained.

"Much better." Sophia smirked, running a finger along the clean bikini line. "Now you're ready for some beach action."

Phoebe shivered at the touch, her nipples hardening. This vacation couldn't come soon enough.

———

"Turn around for me," Sophia ordered as Phoebe stood. "Hmm, just as I thought. Get back here."

Before Phoebe could protest, Sophia's hands were on her ass cheeks, spreading them apart. "Oh honey, this is a whole other situation we need to deal with."

"Sophie!" Phoebe squealed as her friend tugged her cheeks apart even wider.

"Bend over the tub," Sophia commanded, already reaching for the scissors. "Trust me, when you find that hot surfer boy, you'll thank me for cleaning up these spokes."

Phoebe gripped the porcelain, face flushing as she bent

forward. Her breath hitched as Sophia carefully trimmed around her exposed hole.

"Now for the smooth finish," Sophia purred, reaching for the razor and shaving cream. She worked the foam gently around Phoebe's sensitive rim, then drew the razor in careful strokes until every hair was gone. "Stay still, almost done..."

"Unngh," Phoebe moaned softly as Sophia's fingers wiped away the remaining cream with a warm washcloth. Her pussy was wet now, cream building between her swollen lips.

"Perfect!" Sophia declared. Then without warning, she planted a wet kiss right on Phoebe's freshly cleaned hole. "Mwah!"

"Sophie!" Phoebe jerked upright, her whole body tingling as her friend collapsed in giggles.

"Sorry, couldn't resist!" Sophia wheezed between laughs. "You should see your face! But seriously, look how pretty it is now."

Using her phone camera, Phoebe twisted to see her newly smooth backside. Her tight pink hole glistened, completely bare and exposed.

"You're fucking crazy," Phoebe muttered, but couldn't help grinning. Her ass still tingled where Sophia's lips had been.

"You love me," Sophia said, waggling her eyebrows. "Now, let's see that surfer try to resist this perfect little rosebud."

Standing nude before her full-length mirror, Phoebe ran her fingers over her newly groomed mound. The landing strip looked perfect, but as she bent forward and spread herself, she gasped. Sophia had gone further than she realized. Everything from her clit to her ass was completely bare.

"Fuck..." she whispered, grabbing her vanilla body lotion. She poured some into her palm, then slowly slid her hand over the smooth skin. The sensation was electric...no coarse hair, just silky flesh that made her pussy throb with each touch.

Her fingers found her slick entrance, already wet from her exploration. "Mmmm," she moaned softly, working two fingers inside while her other hand continued caressing her bare skin.

With her heart racing, she glanced nervously at her closed door. Then, with trembling hands, she added more lotion to her middle finger. Slowly, she traced it down past her dripping pussy to her tight hole. "Oh god..." she whimpered as she pressed against it.

The tip of her finger slipped inside easily. "Unnngh!" The new sensation made her whole body quiver. She'd never touched herself there before, but now... She pushed deeper, her other hand frantically rubbing her clit.

Her pussy clenched around nothing as she worked her finger in and out of her ass. The forbidden pleasure was overwhelming. Her legs shook as she watched herself in the mirror...spread open, finger buried in her tight hole, face flushed with desire.

"Fuck, fuck, fuck..." she panted, working herself faster until her whole body convulsed in an intense orgasm that left her gripping the edge of the mirror with one hand, trembling from the new discovery. As her vision cleared, she caught movement in the reflection and froze. There was Sophia, leaning against the doorframe with a wicked grin.

"Sophie!" Phoebe spun around, hands flying to cover her face as her whole body flushed crimson.

"Heard some interesting noises," Sophia purred. "Thought I should check on you, but clearly everything is... more than fine. That was hot as fuck, by the way." She bit her lip, eyes dancing. "Almost makes me jealous of that future surfer boy.

In fact..." She stepped closer. "If you can't find someone to properly fuck you on that beach vacation, I might just have to do it myself when you get back."

"Get out!" Phoebe grabbed her pillow and hurled it at her friend's head. Sophia dodged it easily, cackling as she backed out of the room.

"Sweet dreams, baby!" Sophia's laughter echoed down the hall. "Don't forget to wash your hands!"

Phoebe collapsed onto her bed, still naked and trembling, torn between mortification and lingering arousal. Her ass and pussy throbbed with pleasure as Sophia's words echoed in her mind: "I might just have to do it myself..."

The morning sun streamed through the kitchen windows as Phoebe packed the last of her snacks for the bus ride.

"So..." Sophia smirked over her coffee cup. "Sleep well after your little... self-exploration session?"

"Oh my god, shut up," Phoebe groaned, but couldn't hide her smile. "I still can't believe you watched."

"Hey, it was quite the show," Sophia said, then winked as she helped fold the last of Phoebe's sundresses. "At least now I know that ass grooming didn't go to waste."

They hustled Phoebe's bags down to the street, the early morning air still cool. The bus was already idling at the stop.

"Text me when you get there," Sophia said as she pulled Phoebe into a tight hug. Their lips met in a soft, lingering kiss that made Phoebe's stomach flutter. "And keep me updated on all the dirty details."

"I will," Phoebe promised, climbing aboard.

"Find yourself a hot surfer with a big cock!" Sophia called out loudly, making several heads turn. "And if not, remember my offer still stands!"

Phoebe flipped her off through the window, laughing as

the bus pulled away. She watched Sophia's figure grow smaller, her friend still blowing exaggerated kisses. Her pussy tingled thinking about last night, and what adventures might await at the beach.

The memory of Sophia's parting words...and that kiss...lingered as the city faded into the coastal highway. Maybe this vacation would bring more surprises than she'd planned.

The coastal sun was setting as the bus pulled into the small beachside town. Phoebe stretched, working out the kinks from the long ride, spotting a bright yellow Jeep Wrangler with its top down. Leaning against it was a bronze-skinned guy with tousled blond hair, holding a sign with her name.

"Hi, I'm Jake." He flashed a surfer-boy grin that showed off perfect white teeth. His board shorts hung low on narrow hips, and his tank top revealed lean muscle. Cute. Really cute...but those boyish dimples gave away his age. Definitely too young.

"I've got it," Phoebe insisted when he reached for her bags. She struggled with the oversized luggage, definitely overpacked for two weeks, while trying to maintain her dignity in city heels on the loose sand where he'd parked.

"You sure about that?" Jake asked, amusement dancing in his eyes as she wobbled.

"Perfectly f..." Her ankle twisted and she went down hard, landing spread-eagled on top of her bags with a yelp. Sand sprayed everywhere, including up her sundress.

"Right, that's enough of that," Jake said then chuckled, easily hoisting her bags. "First lesson of beach life...lose the heels. You're not in the city anymore."

Her cheeks burning, Phoebe kicked off her shoes, trying not to notice how his muscles flexed as he loaded the Jeep. The warm sand between her toes did feel better.

"You're gonna love this spot," Jake chatted as they wound through town. "Best surfing around, killer sunsets, and the beach is practically private."

The Jeep turned onto a sandy track, and Phoebe's breath caught. There, nestled in the dunes, was her beach cottage for the next two weeks. A weathered blue home with white trim and a wraparound deck. The waves crashed just yards away.

"This is perfect." She breathed out a contented sigh as Jake carried her bags up the wooden steps, still sporting sand in places she'd rather not think about.

"Keys are on the hook inside. I'm usually around town if you need anything." He gave her another dimpled smile before heading back to his Jeep.

Phoebe watched him go, admiring but dismissing. Too young. But standing there on her private deck, feeling the salt breeze on her skin and sand in her panties, she knew the right opportunity would come. This was just the beginning.

"Sophie! Oh my god, this place is amazing!" Phoebe gushed into her phone, wandering through the cottage. The walls were pale blue, decorated with vintage surfboards and nautical artwork. Through the French doors, the ocean stretched endlessly.

"But first, tell me about the hot surfer boy who picked you up," Sophia purred.

"Jake? God, I made such an ass of myself. Fell right on my face in front of him, sand everywhere, including up my..."

"But did you fuck him?" Sophia interrupted.

"What? No! He's like, barely legal. Probably still lives with his parents."

"Mmm, the young ones are the best though." Sophia's voice dripped with suggestion. "They're like Energizer bunnies. Hard, fast, and ready for round two before your first orgasm ends. Plus, they're so eager to please."

"Sophie!" Phoebe laughed, flopping onto the plush white couch. "Not happening. You know my type. Tall, dark, experienced. Preferably old enough to rent a car."

"Oh right, because all that experience has gotten you laid recently?" Sophia snorted. "When was the last time you had a cock that wasn't battery-operated?"

"Fuck off." Phoebe shook her head and grinned. "I'm hanging up now. Going to change and check out the beach."

"Fine, but don't say I didn't warn you about missing out on that young surfer dick!"

Phoebe ended the call, shaking her head again at her friend's one-track mind. She pulled out the white bikini, running her fingers over the fabric. Her freshly smooth pussy tingled at the memory of last night's exploration.

Slipping into the tiny swimsuit, she studied herself in the mirror. The white fabric contrasted softly with her city-pale skin. *Time to work on that tan, and maybe find someone more my type.*

―――

Phoebe grabbed a Corona from the well-stocked fridge, condensation already beading on the clear glass, and gathered her beach supplies. The wooden deck creaked softly under her bare feet as she arranged herself on one of the weathered recliners.

"Perfect," she sighed, cracking open the beer. The first sip fizzed deliciously cold down her throat, washing away the dusty bus journey. She spread the local brochures across her lap, one catching her eye immediately. "Blue Bay Surf School: Private & Group Lessons Available."

"That's it," she murmured, studying the photos of the toned instructors helping students catch waves. If she was going to find her perfect surfer, she needed to understand their world. Plus, the instructor in the main photo had exactly the dark features she preferred.

Setting aside the brochures, she squeezed sunscreen into her palm. The lotion warmed quickly as she worked it over her shoulders and chest, careful not to miss any spots around the tiny white bikini. She smoothed it across her abs and thighs, her hands gliding over her skin with practiced ease.

Adjusting her wide-brimmed hat and designer shades, Phoebe stretched out on the recliner. The late afternoon sun warmed her skin while the salt breeze kept her from overheating. The steady rhythm of the waves already had her feeling drowsy.

"Mmm," she hummed contentedly, taking another long sip of beer. Just a quick rest before dinner. The surfing lessons could wait until tomorrow. Right now, all she needed was this moment of pure beach bliss.

"Mmmhhh..." Phoebe stirred at a deep, rich voice cutting through her doze. Her eyes fluttered open behind her sunglasses to find a bronzed god standing at the edge of her deck.

Dark hair curled damply around his face, water droplets still trailing down his bare chest. Board shorts hung low on cut hip muscles that formed a perfect V disappearing into the waistband. A tribal tattoo wrapped around one biceps, and salt-weathered laugh lines crinkled at the corners of his eyes.

"Huh?" she managed eloquently, still fuzzy from her nap.

"Said you better watch that sun," he said with a smile, his voice like warm honey. "Don't want to burn on your first day here."

Phoebe's brain was too busy drinking in his features to

notice how he knew she'd just arrived. That jaw could cut glass, and his lips... full and curved into a knowing smirk.

Before she could form a coherent response, he was already moving past, continuing his beach walk with long, confident strides. She watched his retreating form, admiring the way his shoulders moved and how the sand clung to his calves.

"Fuck," she whispered, letting her head fall back. Heat bloomed between her thighs just looking at him. If he wasn't interested... well, maybe he had an equally gorgeous brother somewhere nearby. She'd have to ask around town about the mysterious beach walker.

The sun was definitely stronger now...maybe he had a point about burning. But all Phoebe could think about was how his voice had sent shivers down her spine, and how much she wanted to hear it again...preferably while those hands were exploring her body.

"Oh my god, Sophie, you should've seen him," Phoebe gushed into her phone, peeling off her bikini. Her skin was flushed pink where the sun had kissed it. "Like some Greek god just casually strolling past."

"And you just let him walk away?" Sophie scoffed. "Should've been tanning naked, that would've stopped him in his tracks."

"*Ahem!*"

Phoebe spun around, phone dropping to the floor. Jake stood in the doorway, his eyes slowly traveling up her exposed body. His board shorts did nothing to hide his growing reaction.

"I... uh..." He swallowed hard. "Door was open... heard voices... just checking if you needed anything."

Phoebe grabbed for a towel, her heart pounding. The way he was looking at her sent heat flooding between her legs.

"GET THAT YOUNG DICK, PHOEBE!" Sophie's voice blasted from the fallen phone. "WHO CARES ABOUT HIS AGE, JUST FUCK HIM!"

Jake's lips curved into a knowing smile, as he made no move to leave. Instead, he leaned against the doorframe, clearly waiting to see what she'd do next.

Phoebe stood frozen, towel clutched to her chest, suddenly reconsidering every assumption she'd made about younger men. The tension crackled between them as Sophie's words hung in the air.

"I... um..." Phoebe's voice caught in her throat as she watched his tongue dart out to wet his lips.

The ball was in her court now...

―――

Phoebe summoned her willpower. "Thanks, but I have everything I need."

"JUST DO IT!" Sophie's voice boomed from the phone. "Get some now, find Mr. Perfect later!"

Jake's impressive outline strained against his shorts as he waited, one hand casually adjusting himself. Phoebe's mouth went dry.

"No... really, I'm good," she managed, even as her body screamed otherwise. "You should probably go. Before I change my mind."

He lingered. "You sure?"

"Really. Please go." Her voice wavered.

"You know how to reach me." He smirked, giving himself one last suggestive stroke before turning away.

Once he was gone, Phoebe collapsed onto the bed. "Sophie, I'm dying. First you watching my private time, now this! I keep getting caught."

"Did he mind though?"

"God no. He was... very excited. I almost gave in. Fuck, I'll be dreaming about that bulge tonight, pretending it's Beach God instead."

"Should've taken the sure thing while dreaming of Mr. Perfect."

"I need a cold shower," Phoebe groaned. "Talk later."

She hung up and raced to the bathroom, cranking the water to arctic. The icy spray made her squeal and jump, but it did nothing to cool her core temperature or erase the image of Jake's impressive display.

"Cold, cold, cold!" she gasped, letting the shower shock her system. But even as her sunburn cooled, her mind kept replaying the hungry look in Jake's eyes and wondering if she'd made the right choice.

———

The next morning, Phoebe laid out her outfit with purpose. The white bikini top showed just enough cleavage to be noticeable without screaming desperate. The red shorts...thank god she'd ignored Sophie's suggestion of that barely-there thong...hugged her ass perfectly while still being appropriate for actual exercise.

Her heart nearly stopped when she reached the beach meeting point. There he was...Beach God himself, wetsuit pulled down to his waist, explaining technique to the gathering crowd. His abs flexed as he demonstrated the proper stance on a surfboard laid in the sand.

"Welcome, everyone." His voice carried over the waves. "I'm Leon, and I'll be your instructor this week."

The collection of women around her practically vibrated with sexual energy. A blonde in a pink bikini kept flipping her hair, while a redhead somehow needed her sunscreen reapplied every five minutes. Phoebe recognized that hungry look in their eyes...the same one she'd seen in her mirror earlier.

Leon's hands were strong and sure as he adjusted students

seated back on their heels, mimicking the position they'd take on a surfboard. Nearby, their boards remained stacked, waiting for the lesson to begin.

Electricity shot through Phoebe's sex imagining those fingers on her body. She wasn't the only one...a collective sigh went through the group every time he demonstrated a move.

"Remember, ladies, it's all in the hips." He grinned, and Phoebe swore several women actually swooned.

"Focus," she told herself sternly. "You're here to learn surfing, not just ogle the instructor." But as Leon's eyes met hers, a knowing smirk playing on his lips, she realized concentrating might be harder than she'd thought...especially with a dozen other women all imagining the same dirty scenarios she was.

———

"Alright, ladies, let's start with some basic stretches," Leon called out. His hands moved expertly through the group, making minor adjustments to postures.

Phoebe's skin tingled as his warm palms pressed against her lower back. "I'll be gentle," he murmured close to her ear, his breath sending shivers down her spine. "Since you're a bit tender from yesterday's sun."

Her mind flashed back to his warning on her deck. So he had noticed her. Her legs went weak as his fingers traced lightly down her spine, ostensibly correcting her form.

The blonde in the pink bikini practically hissed, her death glare boring into Phoebe. She'd clearly staked her claim early, pressing her chest out whenever Leon passed.

"Good form," Leon's voice rumbled approvingly before moving on, leaving Phoebe struggling to remember how to breathe. Her skin burned where he'd touched her...and not from sunburn.

"Now, reach forward." He demonstrated the next stretch,

muscles rippling. The blonde immediately let out an exaggerated whimper, claiming she needed help with the position.

But Phoebe caught Leon's eyes flickering back to her, that half-smile playing on his lips. The tension crackled between them, even as he went through the motions of helping Pink Bikini.

"Two can play this game," Phoebe thought, arching her back just a little more than necessary for the next stretch. The daggers from the blonde only confirmed she'd hit her mark when Leon's gaze lingered.

"Ladies, select your boards," Leon said, gesturing toward the colorful array laid out on the sand. "They're all beginner-friendly, just different colors."

Phoebe headed for a pink surfboard when a manicured hand shoved her sideways. Pink Bikini Girl muscled in, her artificial tan glowing under the sun.

Irritated and running on instinct, Phoebe pushed back...harder than intended. Pink Bikini sprawled dramatically into the sand with a theatrical "Ow!" that drew everyone's attention.

"Oh god, I'm sorry." Phoebe extended her hand, genuine concern mixing with embarrassment.

Pink Bikini slapped it away, her perfectly made-up face twisting into a sneer. She grabbed the pink board possessively and flounced away, making sure to throw Leon a wounded look.

But Leon seemed suddenly very interested in adjusting the leg strap on his own board, the corner of his mouth twitching. When he finally looked up, his eyes met Phoebe's with barely contained amusement.

Phoebe grabbed a blue board instead, her cheeks burning.

But as she passed Leon, she could have sworn she heard him mutter, "Nice form on that push, too," under his breath.

Pink Bikini shot her another venomous glare, this one promising retribution. But somehow, catching Leon's subtle wink made it all worth it.

———

The lesson ended with everyone sweaty and sandy from practicing pop-ups and stances. As the group dispersed, Phoebe gathered the courage to finally introduce herself to Leon properly.

But Pink Bikini had already pounced. She'd somehow engineered a wardrobe malfunction that left one breast nearly completely exposed, the dark areola peeking out while she giggled and touched Leon's arm.

This time, Leon wasn't looking away. His eyes fixed on Pink Bikini's strategic display as she pressed closer, whispering something that made him laugh.

"Damn," Phoebe muttered, her shoulders slumping. She turned away, not wanting to watch anymore. The walk back to her cottage felt longer than before, the sand dragging at her feet.

She'd thought there had been something there...those knowing looks, the gentle touch, the whispered comment. But apparently, Leon was just as happy with obvious silicone and spray tans as he was with subtle flirtation.

Reaching her deck, she threw her towel aside harder than necessary. Through the palms, she could still see them on the beach. Pink Bikini now practically molded herself to Leon's side.

"Whatever," Phoebe grumbled, heading inside to shower. She had two weeks here. Plenty of time to find someone else. Someone who preferred natural beauty to artificial everything.

But as she stepped under the spray, she couldn't shake the memory of his hands on her back, his breath on her neck... or the bitter disappointment of watching him with someone else.

Fresh from her shower, rivulets of water still trailing down her curves, Phoebe stood wrapped only in a thin towel, as she considered settling in for the night. The holiday package included a well-stocked fridge, and Jake was on call at any time to get anything she needed from the local store. Her nipples tightened against her thin robe as she debated calling him about pizza and wine to drown her sorrows, but then there was a loud rap on the door and his voice calling out, "Jake here, and I'm looking out to sea right now."

She laughed. His shadow through the screen door showed he was deliberately facing away from the cottage.

His deep voice through the door sent a delicious shiver down her spine.

Her nipples hardened against the fabric as she adjusted the towel to ensure it covered her naked body. "What are you doing here, Jake? I was about to call you anyway to see whether I could get takeout pizza or something."

"Better than that," he said, his voice carrying a hint of suggestion that made her pulse quicken. "I can take you to a great little café in town where they have the best pizzas, cocktails, music and even dancing if you like to do that." He paused. "I don't," he added, "but I will take you, and since you don't seem to have anyone else, I can look after you tonight. Maybe even show you around."

Phoebe smiled, heat pooling in her core as she imagined his hands "showing her around." She knew exactly what he was after, and her hardening nipples and dampening thighs told her she wanted the same.

"OK," she said, her voice husky. "What will I wear?"

"It's super casual," he said. "You can wear whatever you like. You'll look spectacular in anything."

"Give me fifteen," she called out, already mentally rifling through her wardrobe. Sophie had packed plenty of "fuck-me" outfits, but maybe something slightly more subtle...

She settled on a gauzy white sundress that showed just enough leg and clung to her curves without being obvious. The thin fabric made wearing a bra impossible...her nipples were clearly visible if the breeze hit just right. Perfect for keeping Jake's attention without screaming desperate.

Running her fingers through her damp curls, she debated makeup before settling on just mascara and lip gloss. Her skin was already glowing from the sun.

"Ready!" She opened the door to find Jake in board shorts and a fitted black t-shirt that showed off his surfer's build. His eyes darkened as they swept over her dress.

"Wow," he breathed. "You look..." He swallowed hard. "Spectacular."

"Spectacular?"

His cheeks flushed but he held her gaze. "Better than spectacular."

The sexual tension from yesterday crackled between them. This time, Phoebe didn't fight it. Maybe Sophie was right. Why not enjoy the eager attention of a younger man? Especially one who looked at her like she was dessert.

"Lead the way," she purred, deliberately brushing against him as she passed. His sharp intake of breath confirmed the dress was doing its job.

The café vibrated with Jimmy Buffett covers and beach party energy. Jake's gentleman act with the car door had Phoebe feeling optimistic about the evening, especially now knowing he was just two years younger.

Then: "Hey, bro!" Jake called out.

Phoebe's stomach dropped. There stood Leon, with Pink Bikini plastered against him in what barely qualified as a dress. The sheer fabric left nothing to the imagination, her enhanced assets on full display as she marked her territory with possessive touches.

Pink Bikini's triumphant smirk said it all as she pressed closer to Leon. "I won," her expression gloated.

"Let's get drinks," Phoebe said quickly, tugging Jake toward the bar. Her earlier disappointment crystallized into determination. To hell with Leon and his obvious taste in women.

She ordered a margarita, then another. The tequila warmed her blood as Jake's hand found the small of her back. His touch was electric, sending shivers up her spine.

When he leaned in to be heard over the music, his lips brushed her ear. "Dance with me?"

I thought he didn't like dancing.

Phoebe turned into his embrace, letting her body melt against his muscled frame. His board shorts did nothing to hide his reaction as she swayed against him.

She'd come here planning to enjoy herself. And with Jake's hungry eyes fixed on her, strong hands spanning her waist, she intended to do exactly that...without sparing another thought for anyone else in the room.

———

The night buzzed with sexual tension as Phoebe caught Leon's unreadable glances. Whatever regret showed in his eyes, she'd made her choice.

The pizza and cocktails left her deliciously uninhibited. Jake's presence became increasingly magnetic as the alcohol coursed through her veins. His hand was on her thigh under the table, his breath hot on her neck when he whispered in her ear. It all built to an unbearable pressure.

"Take me home," she finally breathed, grabbing his wrist. "Now!"

The drive back was torturous. Every bump in the road made her squirm in her seat. Jake's knuckles were white on the steering wheel as he fought to keep his eyes on the road.

By the time they reached her cottage, Phoebe could hardly wait to get inside. She practically dragged Jake up the steps, fumbling with her key, blood pounding in her ears.

The door had just clicked shut behind them when she spun to face him, pupils blown wide with desire.

The gauzy dress clung to her heated skin as Jake crowded her against the wall, his intentions crystal clear in the growing bulge pressing against her hip.

———

Phoebe dropped eagerly, freeing Jake's impressive length from his shorts. She wrapped her lips around him hungrily, savoring his gasp of pleasure when her tongue swirled around his swollen head.

Suddenly her stomach lurched. "Oh fuck!" She bolted for the bathroom.

As violent retching echoed through the door, Jake stood awkwardly, unsure whether to help or leave.

"Don't go!" she called between heaves. "Just... give me a minute."

The toilet flushed, followed by vigorous teeth brushing and mouth gargling. When she emerged naked, her eyes were bright with renewed determination.

"I'm good now," she purred, sauntering toward him. "Those cocktails hit harder than expected."

"You sure?" Jake eyed her with concern.

"Very sure." She nodded, pressing against him. "And I know exactly what will make me feel better..."

Her hand wrapped around his still-hard length as she backed toward the bed, pulling him with her. The hunger in her eyes left no doubt. A little queasiness wasn't going to stop her from getting what she wanted tonight.

"Come here," she said, her breathing ragged, as she spread her legs invitingly. "Show me what you can do with this..."

———

Jake hesitated despite his obvious arousal. "Are you absolutely sure about this?" he said. "You've had quite a few drinks. I don't want you doing anything you'll regret."

"Gimme your phone," Phoebe demanded. "I'll prove how sure I am."

Jake handed it over, watching as she opened the camera app. She held it up, speaking clearly into the lens:

"I, Phoebe Walker, want Jake Surfer-boy." She giggled at not knowing his last name. "To stick this big hard beautiful cock..." She panned down to capture his impressive length, "up my soaking wet, newly trimmed pussy..." The camera moved between her spread legs.

"I am of completely sound mind, and I fucking want this NOW. Hard and fast," she declared firmly. "Before I literally explode from wanting you."

She tossed the phone onto the bed, making sure it was still recording, then rolled onto her back. Her legs spread wide as she used both hands to part her glistening folds.

"Fuck me now, Jake," she demanded. "Please..."

All his hesitation evaporated at the raw need in her voice. The phone captured everything that followed...proving beyond doubt that her enthusiasm was genuine and her consent unmistakable.

"Oh fuck, oh fuck, OH FUCK!" Phoebe's cries escalated with each powerful thrust. Her legs wrapped around Jake's waist, pulling him deeper as the pressure built inside her.

Jake's pace grew frantic, his muscles straining. "I'm getting close," he panted.

"Inside me!" she commanded between moans. "I'm on the pill. Fill me up! I want to feel every drop!"

The raw need in her voice pushed him over the edge. Jake drove into her deep and hard, his balls slapping against her wet skin. With a guttural groan, his cock pulsed as he flooded her. The sensation of his hot release triggered Phoebe's own orgasm.

"FUCK YES!" she screamed, her whole body convulsing. Her pussy spasmed rhythmically around him, milking every last drop as waves of pleasure crashed through her.

Jake collapsed forward, catching himself on his elbows as they both gasped for air. Their eyes met, heavy with post-orgasmic haze. He leaned down for a kiss, but she turned away.

"Not the mouth," she mumbled, remembering her earlier sickness. "But everything else..." Her hands stroked his back appreciatively as their breathing slowly returned to normal.

The forgotten phone had captured it all. Their passionate coupling, her explicit consent, and the mutual satisfaction written across both of their faces.

Jake grabbed the still-recording phone, both of them laughing at the unintentional sex tape they'd created. As he moved to stop the recording, it suddenly buzzed in his hand.

His face dropped instantly as he answered. "Yeah... shit... okay, I'll be right there."

He practically jumped off the bed, gathering his shorts from the floor. The relaxed afterglow vanished, replaced by obvious tension.

"What's wrong?" Phoebe propped herself up on her elbows, his cum still leaking from between her thighs.

"Emergency at work," he said quickly, pulling on his clothes. "I really gotta go."

Something in his tone seemed off...more nervous than concerned. He wouldn't quite meet her eyes as he headed for the door.

"Jake?" she called after him.

"I'll... uh... see you around," he managed before practically running out, leaving Phoebe naked and confused on the messy sheets.

The sudden exit felt wrong, like there was something he wasn't saying. But the alcohol and lingering orgasm made it hard to focus on why.

A dark figure lingered just long enough to see Jake burst out of Phoebe's cottage, fumbling with his shirt as he rushed to his Jeep. The man's face remained hidden in shadow as he slid his phone into his board shorts pocket.

His footsteps were silent in the cool sand as he moved away from Phoebe's hut. The distant sound of Jake's Jeep starting up and peeling out carried across the beach. Inside, Phoebe remained unaware of the observer, still trying to process Jake's abrupt departure.

The figure paused briefly, glancing back at the warm light spilling from Phoebe's windows. His muscled silhouette was briefly illuminated by moonlight before he strode off down the shoreline, waves lapping at his feet as he disappeared into the darkness.

The night breeze carried away any trace of his presence, leaving only questions hanging in the humid air.

Phoebe stared at her phone, Jake's number ringing through to voicemail for the third time. Her head throbbed, a combination of tequila hangover and confused thoughts about last night.

The sheets still smelled like sex and him. She shifted and felt the lingering tenderness between her legs...evidence of how thoroughly he'd fucked her. Despite everything, her body responded to the memory, a warm ache building as she recalled his size, his enthusiasm, the way he filled her completely.

"Fuck," she muttered, pressing her thighs together. The surf lesson started in twenty minutes but the thought of facing either Jake or Leon made her stomach turn. Not to mention Pink Bikini's smug face.

She rolled over, burying her face in the pillow. The sex had been incredible...exactly what she needed. Right up until that phone call.

Who could have called that made him bolt like that? A girlfriend maybe? The thought made her queasy for reasons beyond the hangover. Or was it work like he claimed?

Her phone remained stubbornly silent. No explanatory text, no missed calls, nothing.

"What the hell happened?" she whispered to the empty room. The soreness between her legs reminded her it wasn't a dream, but his hasty exit and current silence suggested she was missing something important.

Something that made him run like he'd seen a ghost.

Sizzle in the SAND

"You're not seriously moping over this guy?" Sophie's voice crackled through the phone. "He was meant to be a vacation fling, remember? Mission accomplished."

Phoebe sighed, watching a gull circle outside her window. "It's not that simple, Soph. The way he left was weird. One minute we're... you know... and the next he's running out like his ass was on fire."

"Details, babe. How was it at least?"

"Amazing," Phoebe admitted, heat rising to her cheeks as she remembered. "Like, mind-blowingly good. Until that phone call..."

"See? You got exactly what you came for. Hot surfer-boy sex. Now go find another one!"

"I'm skipping lessons today. Can't face Leon either after..." She trailed off.

"Retail therapy then," Sophie declared. "Buy something scandalous. Make the next guy's eyes pop out."

Phoebe glanced at Jake's Jeep space, now empty. She'd have to walk into town, but maybe Sophie was right. Sitting there obsessing wouldn't help.

"Fine," she conceded. "But I still want to know what spooked him."

"Less wondering, more shopping," Sophie ordered. "And Phoebe? Next time maybe ease up on the tequila first."

———

"What the fuck were you thinking?" Leon cornered Jake in the equipment shed, his voice low and dangerous. "She's a fucking guest, Jake. A PAYING guest."

Jake busied himself with the surfboards, avoiding Leon's glare. "I don't know what you're..."

"Don't." Leon slammed his hand against the wall. "Don't even try denying it. The whole fucking beach heard you two last night. Mrs. Peterson next door called to complain about the noise."

Jake's face flushed red. "She wanted..."

"I don't care if she begged for it!" Leon cut him off. "You're staff. She's a guest. This isn't some fucking hookup bar."

"But you and Tan..."

"That's different and you know it." Leon stepped closer, forcing Jake to look at him. "You're done with her. You hear me? No private lessons, no more errands, no more anything. Stay the fuck away from Phoebe."

Jake's jaw set, but he nodded, knowing he'd crossed a line.

"I mean it, Jake. One more incident like this and you're out. I don't care how good an instructor you are." Leon's voice carried the weight of authority. "Now get the beginner class ready. And Jake? Delete her number."

"Hello?" Phoebe's heart leaped when the call connected, then plummeted at the unfamiliar female voice.

"This isn't Jake. I'm Lily. I'll be handling your needs and activities for the remainder of your stay."

"Oh." Phoebe's throat tightened. "Is Jake okay? Did something happen?"

"He's fine," Lily responded, too smoothly. "Just a routine roster change. Nothing to worry about. Can I help you with anything?"

The casual dismissal in Lily's tone made Phoebe's stomach knot. Less than twelve hours ago Jake was inside her, making her scream his name. Now he'd been erased like he never existed.

"No... I..." Phoebe swallowed hard. "I was actually calling to cancel my lessons."

"Of course. I'll mark that down. Anything else?"

"Yeah," Phoebe said, anger replacing confusion. "Tell Jake he's a fucking coward."

She hung up before Lily could respond, throwing her phone onto the bed. "Routine roster change" her ass. Something happened after that call last night, and she was starting to think she knew exactly who made it.

———

"Hi... Lily? It's Phoebe again. Sorry about before..." She forced cheerfulness into her voice. "I actually could use a favor. Any chance of a lift into town? I'm feeling like retail therapy."

"Of course!" Lily's response was bright and professional, as if Phoebe's earlier outburst never happened. "I can be there in about fifteen minutes if that works?"

"Perfect, thanks." Phoebe started gathering her things, stomach churning with mixed emotions. Maybe this Lily knew what happened with Jake. At the very least, a friendly face might help clear her head.

Just yesterday Jake was opening car doors for her, looking at her with those hungry eyes. Now he was gone without explanation, replaced by this mysteriously cheerful Lily.

Through her window, she spotted a resort vehicle pulling up all too soon. She changed into a sundress, wincing slightly at the pleasant ache between her legs...a reminder of last night's passion. *What was that?* The evidence of Jake's enthusiasm was still dried on her so she quickly sponged her inner thighs and spritzed a little perfume between her legs and under her arms. No time for a shower.

Time to paste on a smile and pretend last night never happened.

———

As Phoebe emerged from the bathroom, still slightly damp from her hasty cleanup, she found Lily standing in her cottage...a striking contrast to Jake's tall, muscled frame that had filled this same space last night.

The petite redhead looked like she stepped out of a resort brochure, her flowing sundress matching the hibiscus tucked behind her ear. Her smile seemed genuine, but there was something knowing in her green eyes that made Phoebe wonder exactly what she'd heard about last night's events.

"Ready for some shopping?" Lily chirped, jingling her car keys.

"Thanks for doing this," Phoebe managed, gathering her purse. The smell of sex still lingered in the room. Surely Lily could smell it too? But the redhead's professional smile never wavered.

Walking to the car, Phoebe's thighs reminded her of Jake's vigorous attention. She slid into the passenger seat, hyper-aware of the lingering tenderness. Just hours ago she was begging him to cum inside her. Now she was making small talk with his replacement like nothing happened.

"So... this roster change," Phoebe ventured carefully. "It was rather sudden."

Lily kept her eyes on the road. "Well, there was an incident last night. Jake broke some pretty serious rules about guest interactions."

"Oh?" Phoebe tried to sound casual, but heat crept up her neck.

"Mhmm." Lily glanced sideways, a smile playing at her lips. "Apparently the whole beach heard him breaking those rules. Very... enthusiastically."

Phoebe's face burned crimson as she remembered her own loud cries of pleasure. She stared out the window, mortified.

"Mrs. Peterson next door was particularly emphatic about the... vocal nature of the incident," Lily added with deliberate emphasis.

"Right." Phoebe sunk lower in her seat, suddenly very interested in the passing scenery. She pressed her thighs together unconsciously, remembering exactly how "enthusiastic" things had gotten.

Lily's smile widened, but she mercifully changed the subject to shopping recommendations, leaving Phoebe to silently relive every scream and moan that had apparently carried across the beach.

They browsed through racks of sundresses, Lily proving to be surprisingly good company. Over iced coffees at a beachfront café, Phoebe finally worked up the courage to ask about Leon and Pink Bikini Girl.

"Tanya." Lily rolled her eyes. "Complete psycho. She dated Leon last season and never accepted it was over. Shows up regularly, causes scenes, tries to make other female guests miserable."

"She seemed... territorial," Phoebe admitted, remembering those hostile glares.

"Oh honey, you have no idea." Lily leaned in closer. "She actually got banned from the resort twice. But her daddy's a big investor there, so she keeps coming back. Leon's too nice to get a restraining order, but she's seriously unhinged."

"That explains a few things..." Phoebe thought about Leon's strange behavior...his distance.

"Watch your back with her," Lily warned, stirring her coffee. "Tanya's got this thing about any woman Leon shows interest in. And trust me, it's pretty obvious he's noticed you."

"Noticed me...?" Phoebe's heart skipped a beat.

Lily smirked knowingly. "I've worked here long enough to

know the signs. Leon's not exactly subtle when he's interested. Tanya knows it too, and she doesn't take kindly to competition. Just... be careful. She fights dirty when she's jealous."

Phoebe absorbed this, remembering Pink Bikini's... Tanya's... predatory smile during lessons. Suddenly Leon's hot-and-cold attitude made more sense.

———

"So... Leon's interested in me?" Phoebe echoed, trying to sound casual while examining another rack of bikinis.

"Girl, please." Lily snorted. "I've seen that look before."

Phoebe's cheeks flushed. "What look?"

"The one he gave you," Lily said, grinning.

Phoebe froze. "Wait... how did you...?"

"You didn't even notice I was in the group, did you?" Lily smirked. "You were too busy drooling over Leon to see anyone else."

"I was not!" Phoebe protested.

"Uh huh." Lily smirked. "And I suppose you weren't checking out his ass in those board shorts either?"

"I... that's not..." Phoebe stuttered, remembering exactly how good Leon looked.

"The sexual tension between you two was thick enough to cut with a knife," Lily continued mercilessly. "Though after last night's performance with Jake, maybe you're working through it in other ways..."

"Oh god," Phoebe groaned, burying her face in a sundress. "Can we pretend that never happened?"

"Sure." Lily laughed. "But honey? Leon definitely heard it too. His cottage isn't far from yours."

Phoebe's mortification reached new heights as she realized Leon might have heard every moan, every cry, every time she screamed Jake's name.

"You really think he might have heard?"

"Oh, sweetie." Lily's voice dropped to a whisper as they browsed a jewelry stand. "Leon's the one who caught Jake. He's the one who made the roster change."

Phoebe froze again, a shell necklace slipping from her fingers. "He... what?"

"Leon heard everything last night. And I mean everything." Lily gave her a pointed look. "He's the one who called Jake's phone."

The pieces suddenly clicked into place—the phone call, Jake's abrupt exit, and his silence since then. "That's why he ran out so fast..."

"Mhmm. Leon was... let's say 'not happy' about one of his instructors fucking a guest." Lily paused. "Especially that particular guest."

"What do you mean 'that particular'...?"

"Come on, Phoebe. Leon's got it hard for you already. Then he hears you screaming Jake's name half the night?" Lily shook her head. "Trust me, Jake's lucky he only got reassigned."

Phoebe's stomach churned with embarrassment and something else...the thought of Leon listening to her pleasure, hearing every moan, every beg for Jake to cum inside her.

———

The drive back was quiet. Phoebe was lost in thoughts of Leon, Jake, and last night's passionate mistake. As Lily was parking the car she broke the silence. "Do you want me to book a private lesson with Leon?"

Phoebe's heart skipped a beat. "You think that's a good idea?"

"I do." Lily said. "And I know him better than anyone."

"Oh..." Phoebe's face fell slightly, imagining Lily as another notch in Leon's bedpost, another beautiful woman who'd felt those strong hands on her body.

Catching Phoebe's expression, Lily burst out laughing. "I'm his half-sister, Phoebe!"

"His... oh!" Relief flooded through her, followed by embarrassment. After another moment of silence, Phoebe said, "But after last night... with Jake..." Her voice trailed off.

"Look." Lily turned in her seat. "Leon's proud. And yes, hearing you with Jake probably stung. But I know my brother. Trust me, I'm well aware of the effect my brother has on women. But you're different, Phoebe. I feel like you two might be right for each other. And well, while you might have gone in the wrong direction last night..." Lily raised her eyebrows. "Today is another day."

Phoebe fidgeted with her shopping bags. "So you really think I should book a lesson?"

"I think," Lily said carefully, "that life's too short for regrets. And I happen to know Leon has no lessons scheduled tomorrow morning."

"But what about Tanya?"

"Let me worry about psycho Barbie." Lily's green eyes sparkled. "So... should I book that lesson?"

Phoebe's mind flooded with images of Leon's muscled torso, his intense gaze, those strong hands adjusting her stance on the board...

"Do it," she decided, forcing a smile. "Before I lose my nerve."

"Perfect." Lily grabbed her phone, but then she hesitated and grinned slyly. "Oh, and Phoebe? Maybe keep the volume down this time. Mrs. Peterson's heart can only take so much excitement."

Phoebe laughed nervously, her cheeks flushing as Lily dialed. The laughter faded, though, when Lily said into the phone, "Oh, hi, Lynn. Why are you answering Leon's phone?"

Phoebe's stomach twisted as Lily's expression changed instantly. The lines between her brows deepened, and her usual confidence slipped away.

"Yes. I'm on my way," Lily said, her voice strained.

Phoebe leaned closer, her heart pounding. "What is it?" Phoebe asked.

Lily's lips trembled as she tried to form the words. "Leon's at the hospital. Some kind of accident. They... they don't know what happened."

Lily started the car again and glanced at Phoebe, her expression questioning whether she was coming or staying. Phoebe nodded, latched her seatbelt, and the two sped off toward the hospital.

———

The drive to the hospital was a blur of screeching tires and Lily's white-knuckled grip on the steering wheel. Phoebe's heart hammered in her chest, as thoughts of Leon lying in the hospital flooded her mind. The worry was overwhelming. What had happened to him?

"Fuck," Lily muttered, swerving around a slow-moving van. Her fitted tank top showed the tension in her shoulders. "That idiot Lynn couldn't give me details."

They screeched into the hospital parking lot, Lily's tires throwing gravel. Phoebe's breasts heaved with each anxious breath as they rushed through automatic doors. The antiseptic smell hit her nostrils, making her feel like throwing up.

"I'm looking for Leon Matthews," Lily demanded at reception, her voice tight.

"Room 204," the receptionist said. "But family only."

"I'm his sister," Lily snapped, already moving. She glanced back at Phoebe. "Coming?"

Phoebe nodded, following Lily down the hallway. As they approached room 204, wondering what state they'd find Leon in, he stepped out into the corridor looking as fit, strong and sexy as ever. His bare chest rippled under a half-buttoned shirt; a few scratches visible but nothing serious. Phoebe's nipples hardened at the sight of him. Somehow he looked even more ruggedly handsome than before. Her thighs pressed together instinctively as she watched his muscles flex when Lily flew into his arms.

"You idiot!" Lily sobbed into his broad chest, her tears dampening his shirt. "We thought... Lynn didn't know..."

"I'm OK. Just a few scrapes from a rogue wave. But..." His deep voice resonated through Phoebe's core.

Leon's dark eyes met Phoebe's over his sister's head, that familiar heat making the walls of her pussy flutter. His gaze lingered on her flushed face before returning to Lily. "It's Jake."

Lily pushed back. "What about Jake?"

Phoebe shifted her weight. Her cheeks burned under Leon's intense scrutiny.

"He broke his leg, Lil," he said, still holding his sister but his eyes locked on Phoebe's parted lips. "Though I'm touched by the cavalry, it's for him not me."

"Is he in..." Lily nodded toward the door, "there?"

Leon stood aside so Lily could enter. His mouth quirked up in that devastating half-smile that made Phoebe's core flood with need. "You want to check he hasn't damaged something else?" he asked Phoebe, his voice husky.

She shook her head and sank into a nearby seat. "Will he be OK?"

"He's tough," Leon said. "He never makes a fuss."

"Oh. Good."

"Yeah. You wouldn't know he'd even broken his leg. No screaming or shouting." His words dripped with innuendo.

Phoebe flushed at the reference, heat rising to her cheeks. "Listen, Leon..."

He held his hand up. "No need for explanations. You were

both free to do what you liked. But maybe now he'll be out of action for a while. You might need to try some other moves." His eyes darkened with desire.

"Please, Leon. I thought you were taken."

"Taken?"

"Tanya."

"Oh fuck... No way. No fucking way. Really?"

"Well, it certainly looked like it. She was all over you at the café. And you looked like you were enjoying the view."

"I was enjoying the view of you until you decided to throw it down with my brother."

"Jake's your brother?"

"Yeah."

"And Lily's your sister?"

"Half-sister."

"Any other siblings?"

"Why? You want to fuck someone else while Jake's out of action?"

Phoebe shot up, her breasts heaving with anger. "Fuck you, Leon. Tell Jake I hope he gets better fast. And tell him I'm happy to give him the blowjob he never got last time. We can do that while his leg is in plaster."

She started to storm away when his strong hand gripped her arm. Heat radiated from where his skin touched hers. She tried to pull away, but he held fast until she stopped and dropped her shoulders. As she stood facing away, he moved in front of her, bent down and claimed her mouth in a searing kiss that made her knees weak.

"Can I take his place?" Leon growled against her lips.

Instead of answering, she rose on her tiptoes, grabbed his face and crushed her mouth to his. Her tongue slid between his lips, tasting him as her pussy dripped with need. His hard length pressed against her stomach as the kiss deepened, promising so much more to come.

Phoebe sank into the hard plastic chair again, her thighs pressing together as Leon's scent lingered around her. "Can I borrow your phone?" he asked, his deep voice making her nipples tighten against her dress. "Need to update Lynn."

She handed it over, watching his strong fingers wrap around the device. Pleasure radiated from her center remembering those hands positioning her on the surfboard. Leon stepped away to make the call, but not before his knuckles grazed her bare shoulder, sending electricity through her body.

While Lily was in with Jake, Phoebe couldn't help stealing glances at Leon's muscled back as he spoke quietly into the phone. His shirt still hung half-open, revealing tantalizing glimpses of his scratched but perfect chest. She shifted in her seat, her panties growing damp just watching him move.

Lily emerged looking relieved, her green eyes bright. "Clean break," she announced. "He'll be fine in no time." She glanced between Phoebe and Leon, who had just finished his call. "So... about that lesson tomorrow with Leon? Still interested?" she asked Phoebe.

Phoebe's breath caught as Leon turned, his dark eyes meeting hers with an intensity that made her core throb. That devastating half-smile played across his lips as he gave a slow, deliberate nod. Her nipples hardened instantly at the promise in his gaze.

"Yes," Phoebe breathed, barely able to form words as Leon approached. He handed her phone back, then bent down. His lips brushed the top of her head, sending shivers down her spine. The brief contact left her pussy aching for more as he disappeared back into Jake's room.

"Perfect!" Lily clapped, clearly delighted. But Phoebe barely heard her, lost in thoughts of tomorrow's lesson... Leon's strong hands on her body, the water cooling her heated skin, his intense gaze... She pressed her thighs together as anticipation built like a wave ready to break.

Phoebe stood naked before the mirror, her heart racing as she reached for the skimpy black bikini she and Sophie had giggled over in the shop. The tiny triangles of fabric made her already hard nipples more prominent as she tied them in place, adjusting until her full breasts were perfectly lifted and displayed.

"Fuck," she whispered, turning to examine the back. The thin string disappeared between her ass cheeks. She bent slightly, watching how the minimal coverage shifted, barely concealing her tight asshole. She could see her butthole spokes radiating out from behind the string and her pussy throbbed as she imagined Leon's reaction... his dark eyes taking in every exposed inch of skin while he "adjusted her stance."

The bottoms sat high on her hips, the front triangle barely covering her landing strip. When she moved, the fabric pulled snug against her pussy lips, creating a delicious friction that made her wetness gather. Perfect for driving him crazy, she thought with a smirk.

Reaching for the sheer white sarong, she wrapped it around her hips, the gauzy material clinging to her curves while providing just enough modesty for the walk to their meeting spot. The contrast between the transparent fabric and the black bikini underneath was striking.

Her nipples tightened further as she imagined his strong hands undoing the sarong's knot, those fingers grazing her hip bone. She tossed her beach towel and water into her bag, already wet with anticipation of what the "lesson" might bring.

The morning sun warmed her exposed skin as she hurried

along the beach, the string of her bikini creating exquisite tension with each step. Her sex rippled with need, imagining how easily Leon could push the thin fabric aside when the moment finally came.

Leon stood at the water's edge, board shorts riding low on his hips as Phoebe approached. The sunlight highlighted every muscle, every line of his torso that she'd tried so hard not to stare at during her first and only lesson.

"You came," he said simply, his expression unreadable.

"Not yet," she said, "but very soon. I hope."

Leon's dark eyes blazed at her boldness, his jaw tightening as he took in her barely covered body. "That sarong's nice," he said, voice rougher than before.

"Want me to take it off?" Phoebe's fingers toyed with the knot at her hip, her nipples visibly hard through the tiny black triangles. His gaze dropped to her chest, lingering.

"Depends if you're here for a real lesson," he growled, stepping closer. The ocean spray misted his abs, making them glisten. "Or something else."

Phoebe untied the sarong, letting it flutter to the sand. Leon's nostrils flared as he saw just how little the black bikini covered. "Both," she breathed, watching his board shorts tighten at the front. "I want to learn everything you can teach me."

"Fuck," he muttered, his eyes traveling down her body. "Turn around. Let me see your... stance."

She did as he asked. Heat flooding her core as she felt his hungry gaze on her nearly-bare ass. Water lapped near their feet as he moved behind her, close enough that she could feel his body heat.

"Your position needs work," he said hoarsely, his large hands gripping her hips. His thumbs brushed the strings of her bikini, making her pussy clench with need. "Let me show you how to ride it properly."

"The board or something else?" she asked, pressing back against his growing hardness.

"Not the board," he whispered, his hot breath on her ear making her shiver. His rough hands slid up her ribs, fingers finding her nipples through the thin fabric. She moaned as he pinched them, her knees weakening as pleasure shot straight to her core.

"Pick up your stuff and follow me," he commanded, his voice dark with promise.

"Where are we going?" Her pussy throbbed at the authority in his tone.

He pointed toward the distant headland. "Just around that corner. Gull Bay."

"What's there?"

"Gulls. Nesting," he said with a wicked grin. "They make so much fucking noise that no one will hear you screaming when I make you cum harder than you ever have before."

"Cum?" she breathed, feeling her juices coating her inner thighs.

"Multiple times," he growled, pulling her against his chest. "I'm not just an expert at surfing. And I've been thinking about tasting you since that first lesson."

Need coiled tight within her, wetness now visibly darkening the thin strip of her bikini bottom. Without another word, she grabbed her bag, desperate to follow him to their private cove.

They rounded the corner into Gull Bay, secluded and empty except for the screeching birds overhead. Leon took her beach bag, dropping it on the warm sand. His dark eyes devoured her as he stepped close, untying her bikini top with skilled fingers. Her breasts sprang free, nipples tightening in the sea breeze.

"Beautiful," he murmured, sliding the strings of her thong down her thighs. His thumb traced the neat strip of dark hair above her pussy. "Love this little landing strip. So fucking sexy."

She trembled as his thick finger slid through her trimmed pubes, then dipped between her slick folds. "Mmm, already dripping for me," he growled, adding a second finger and coating them in her juices. Her pussy throbbed around him as he withdrew, bringing his glistening fingers up to his mouth. "Sweet as I imagined."

Phoebe watched, breathless and motionless, as he stripped off his board shorts. Her eyes widened at his massive cock, already thickening against his thigh. The smooth, hairless skin made it look even bigger.

"In the water first for a swim," he said with a wicked grin, grabbing her hand. She yelped as he pulled her toward the waves, both of them diving under the first breaker.

"Fuck!" she squealed, surfacing with a gasp. The cold water had her nipples painfully hard, but the heat between her legs only intensified as Leon's wet, naked body pressed against hers.

"Just wait," he promised darkly. "You'll be hot soon enough." His cock, now fully hard, nudged against her ass as the waves rocked them together.

———

"Are you going to fuck me right here in the ocean?" she asked, grinding back against his hardness.

"Got other plans for you," he growled, nipping her earlobe. He guided her back to shore, their wet bodies glistening in the sun. Water droplets rolled down her curves as he spread their towels meticulously on the warm sand.

"On your hands and knees," he commanded. She complied eagerly, pussy pulsing at his authoritative tone. His large

Sizzle in the SAND

palm pressed between her shoulder blades, guiding her face down to the towel while keeping her ass raised high. A light tap on her inner thighs made her spread them wider.

"Unnghh!" she moaned as his hot tongue circled her tight ring of muscle. Her whole body shuddered as he rimmed her thoroughly, his skilled mouth making her writhe. His hands gripped her ass cheeks, spreading them wider as he delved deeper.

"Fuck... Leon!" she cried out, fisting the towel as his tongue pushed inside her sensitive hole. Her pussy dripped onto the towel beneath her as he ate her ass with passionate intensity. The gulls' cries overhead masked her increasingly desperate moans as he reduced her to a quivering mess.

His stubble scratched deliciously against her sensitive skin while his tongue worked magic, making her arch and push back against his face shamelessly. "Please..." she whimpered, not even sure what she was begging for anymore.

Her fingers found her swollen clit, rubbing frantically from side to side as pleasure built higher. "Fuck... don't stop," she gasped as his tongue probed deeper into her ass. Her juices coated her hand as she worked herself closer to the edge.

"Unnnghhhh... FUCK!" she screamed as his tongue pushed firmly against her pulsing ring. Her whole body trembled violently as the most intense orgasm of her life crashed through her. Her pussy gushed, soaking the towel beneath her as she bucked and writhed.

"LEON... OH GOD... LEONNN!" Her legs shook uncontrollably as waves of pleasure made her collapse forward. Still his talented tongue worked her spasming hole while aftershocks wracked her frame. She could hear the gulls screeching overhead but her own cries of ecstasy drowned them out.

Her pussy continued to pulse and drip as she slowly came down, gasping for air. Her fingers were still pressed against her throbbing clit as the final tremors subsided. "Holy... fuck..." she panted, her whole body limp with satisfaction.

Leon kissed his way up her spine, his hard cock pressing against her soaked pussy. "That was just the warm-up," he growled in her ear.

"I could munch on that tight little ray of sunshine for the rest of my life," he growled as she rolled onto her back, her body glistening with sweat and seawater on the drenched towel.

"Fuck me, Leon," she begged, spreading her legs wide. "I need your cock in me. NOW!"

His massive shaft was already rock-hard as she pulled her knees up to her chest, exposing her dripping pussy. He slid into her in one smooth thrust, making her cry out as he filled her completely. His hips pistoned frantically, his cock plunging deep with each powerful stroke.

"Unnghh... FUCK!" she screamed as another orgasm ripped through her, her pussy gushing around his thick shaft. "Cum inside me! Please... fill me up... CUM IN ME!"

Her desperate pleas pushed him over the edge. With a primal roar, his cock pulsed violently, pumping load after massive load deep into her greedy cunt. "PHOEBE!" he bellowed as he kept cumming, his hot seed overflowing and running down her ass.

"Yes... yes... so much cum," she moaned, her pussy milking every drop from his throbbing cock. Her walls continued to spasm around him as he finally finished emptying himself inside her.

They collapsed together on the wet towel, panting heavily as the waves crashed nearby. "Fuck," he breathed against her neck. "That was incredible."

———

"Let me give you the best blowjob of your life," Phoebe purred, but Leon shook his head with a wicked grin.

"Sit on my face first," he commanded. She hesitated, feeling their combined fluids trickling down her thighs. His eyes darkened with lust. "I want to taste us together."

The raw sexuality of his request made her pussy throb anew. She straddled his face, watching in awe as he eagerly licked their mingled juices. His tongue delved deep inside her, cleaning every drop while her trimmed strip of hair tickled his nose.

"Fuck... LEON!" she cried as he sucked her sensitive clit. His strong hands found her breasts, pinching and rolling her nipples as she arched back, bracing herself on his muscular thighs. She ground against his talented mouth, riding his face with abandon.

Fresh waves of pleasure rippled through her trembling center, her body already tensing for another devastating peak. His tongue worked magic on her swollen clit while he devoured their combined essence. "I'm gonna... OH GOD!" she screamed as she exploded, gushing into his eager mouth and across his face.

The gulls screeched overhead, the waves crashed on the shore, and Phoebe's cries of ecstasy echoed off the cliffs as pleasure consumed her. Leon gripped her hips tightly, drinking down every drop as her body convulsed in the most intense climax yet.

She finally collapsed beside him, both of them panting heavily as the ocean spray cooled their burning skin. His face glistened with the evidence of her pleasure as he smiled wickedly. "Now about that blowjob..."

"Shit... company," Leon muttered, propping himself up on his elbows. A couple emerged around the rocky point, still distant but heading their way. Phoebe quickly grabbed her black bikini bottoms; the thin strings were still damp as she tied them. Her nipples tightened in the breeze as she decided to leave her top off, feeling deliciously wanton.

Leon pulled on his board shorts.

"Later," she promised with a sultry wink, helping Leon up. "After dinner at the café, I'll show you what else my mouth can do."

They dove into the waves, the cool water washing away their passionate encounter. As they emerged, rivulets running down their bodies, the approaching couple smiled and waved. The woman's eyes lingered appreciatively on Leon's muscled chest while her partner openly admired Phoebe's bare breasts.

"Beautiful day," the woman called out as they passed. Phoebe felt a thrill of exhibitionist pleasure at their admiring gazes.

She finally tied on her top and wrapped the sheer sarong around her hips while Leon packed their beach bag. Glancing back, she saw the couple now stripped naked, running into the surf. Their uninhibited joy made her smile, remembering her own wild abandon just minutes before.

"Tonight," she whispered in Leon's ear as they left, making his board shorts twitch, "I'm going to make you cum so hard you'll forget your name."

They rounded the corner to find Tanya waiting, her face contorting with rage. "You fucking bastard!" she screamed at Leon. "I knew something was going on!"

Leon raised his hands. "Tanya, calm down. It's over between us..."

"SHUT UP!" She lunged at Phoebe, grabbing a fistful of wet hair before Leon could yank her away. Undeterred, Tanya charged again, ripping away Phoebe's sarong and bikini bottom in one violent motion.

"Ha! Look at that!" Tanya pointed at Phoebe's exposed landing strip. "Your little bush babe missed the memo about waxing."

SMACK! Phoebe's palm connected with Tanya's cheek, sending her sprawling onto the sand. As she scrambled up for another attack, Phoebe calmly retied her bikini bottom.

"You wanna know what this is?" Phoebe gestured to her pubic hair, voice dripping with venom. "That was Leon's mustache about thirty minutes ago."

"You fucking BITCH!" Tanya lunged again but Leon's hand pressed firmly against her chest, holding her back.

"You're not going to touch her. Ever again," he growled.

Phoebe stepped closer, eyes blazing. "And if you try, I'll rip those fucking clip-ons off your chest."

Tanya staggered to her feet, sand clinging to her designer bikini. "That's it! I'm done with you for good, Leon! You'll never get your hands on this body again!"

"Thank Christ for that!" he shouted at her retreating back.

Turning to Phoebe, he whistled low. "Wow, where the fuck did that come from?"

She shrugged, adjusting her top. "There's more to me than screaming orgasms."

His cock twitched visibly in his shorts. "I'm definitely looking forward to finding out what else."

Phoebe was curled against Leon on the sofa, sharing the last slice of pizza when her phone buzzed. Her face lit up seeing Sophie's name.

"Hey, Soph!" Her smile faded quickly as she sat upright. "Wait, what? When? ... No, you're not interrupting anything... Well yes, but..." She shot Leon an apologetic look as she listened. "Sweetie, you should have called right away..."

Leon watched concern deepen on Phoebe's face as she talked. When she finally ended the call, she slumped back against the cushions.

"What's wrong?" he asked, running his fingers along her arm.

"Sophie lost her job. Said she didn't want to call in case I was 'doing something.'"

"Doing someone," Leon corrected with a smirk.

"Not helpful," Phoebe scoffed, but couldn't hide her smile. "She's completely distraught. I don't know whether to stay here or go home..."

"Ask her to come stay here," Leon said without hesitation.

"Where?"

"In your cottage. And if she needs space to herself, you can stay at mine." His gaze smoldered with intent. "We can finally test how soundproof those walls are."

"You're serious?" Phoebe searched his face.

"Of course. Call her back."

"You're kind of amazing, you know that?" She reached for her phone, then paused. "You sure? Did you need to ask your boss whether she can share my place?"

"I am the boss." Leon grinned, pulling Phoebe close for a deep kiss before she could dial. "This is a family business. My family."

"What? You... and Lily?"

"And Jake. Our parents died in a car accident five years ago and we inherited all of this."

"But Lily said that Tanya's..."

"Yeah, her dad was in partnership with my parents. He holds 50%. But he's a great guy. Not like her."

"Oh!" Phoebe's mind raced with this new information.

"I'll tell you everything after we sort Sophie out."

"OK, done and then I can give you that blowjob I

promised." Her sex throbbed at the memory of his tongue licking their combined juices from her folds.

"I'd like that," he growled, his cock already stirring.

"Me too. I LOVE sucking cock." The words tumbled out before she could stop them. Her cheeks flushed at her wanton admission.

"But only mine, right?" His voice held a hint of possessiveness that made her shiver.

"Of course," she whispered, already imagining taking his massive length down her throat. "Only yours."

She quickly dialed Sophie before the heat between them could derail their plans entirely.

"She's coming," Phoebe announced, ending the call with a sultry grin. "And so can you."

She knelt between his legs, taking his thick shaft deep into her throat in one smooth motion. Her nose pressed against his groin as her tongue snaked out to lap at his balls. Leon groaned as she worked him expertly, her throat muscles massaging his length while she hummed with pleasure.

"Fuck... gonna cum..." he growled. She pulled back, tongue extended as his cock erupted, painting it with thick ropes of cum before she swallowed with a satisfied "Mmm... yum."

Later, curled together on the sofa, Phoebe mused, "I think Jake will love Sophie. She's really outgoing. I've known her forever. She needs a good guy now that I've found mine."

"Found yours?"

"Yeah. I know my job's back home but... I want to see where this goes. If you're willing."

"Willing? Fuck yeah." He traced patterns on her arm. "What exactly is your job?"

"Event planner."

"Perfect timing. Lynn wants to retire, and we need someone with those exact skills to run this place."

"Me? Run this?"

"Why not? You'd be here permanently. Plus I could fuck the staff without firing myself." He winked.

"I'd need to consider Sophie but... if she's settled and nearby... Yes!"

"Yes?"

"Yes, yes, yes, yes, yes."

He laughed. "Maybe we can find something for her too."

Phoebe squealed. "Really?"

"We'll see. I just want you happy. That makes me happy."

"Is this moving too fast?"

"No. Mom and Dad worked so hard and then one day..." His eyes welled up. "They'd love you, Phoebe. I love you, Phoebe."

"I love you too, Leon. We just met but... it feels like we're soulmates."

Leon pulled Phoebe closer, kissing her tears away as emotion overwhelmed them both. His hand slid under her t-shirt, cupping her breast as their kisses deepened with renewed passion.

"Mmmmh, again?" she murmured against his lips. "After everything today?"

"Can't get enough of you," he growled, pinching her nipple. "Never enough."

A knock at the door jolted them from their morning doze. "Shit—Sophie!" Phoebe scrambled to fix her rumpled clothes.

"Already?" Leon tugged his shorts on.

"Must've caught the first bus after we talked." Phoebe opened the door to Sophie's tear-stained face, mascara trails marking her cheeks as she clutched an overnight bag.

"Oh, honey," Phoebe enveloped her in a tight hug as Sophie's shoulders shook with fresh sobs.

"I'm sorry... everything's just so fucked up and..." Sophie stopped short, spotting Leon. Her red-rimmed eyes widened. "Oh! You must be the reason for all the screaming at the bay."

Leon shot Phoebe a look.

"I tell her everything." Phoebe shrugged.

"Everything?"

"Pretty much."

"Well, to be truly accurate, the screaming started with my brother." Leon smirked.

"Can we not go there?" Phoebe blushed while Leon laughed.

Sophie gave Leon an appraising look before mimicking, "Leon... OH GOD, LEON!" Her impression was eerily accurate.

"Jesus Christ." Phoebe covered her face. "Please stop."

"Perfect timing for me to head out." Leon grabbed his keys, grinning. "You two catch up. Phoebe can fill you in on... everything she's missed telling you." He kissed Phoebe deeply, then surprised Sophie with a warm hug. "Call me later?" he said to Phoebe as he walked through the door.

After he left, Sophie collapsed on the sofa.

"Spill everything," Phoebe demanded. "What happened with the job?"

"Had another run-in with Marsha."

"Again?"

"Yeah, she's always had it in for me. It finally came to a head and since she calls the shots..." Sophie shrugged helplessly.

Phoebe grabbed a bottle of wine. "You might need this. But I have news that could make your day."

"I'll take anything right now."

"Well, Leon's offered me a manager position here... and,"

Phoebe rushed on as Sophie's face fell, "he might have a permanent spot for you too."

"Really?"

"Yeah! I told him about your skills. You'll at least get a chance to prove yourself. And I know you will."

Sophie launched herself at Phoebe. "We'll still be together!"

"We will! And look..." Phoebe showed her phone displaying Jake's photo.

"Who's this?"

"Jake. Hot, right?"

"Yeah, he's hot." Sophie's lukewarm response surprised Phoebe, but she chalked it up to emotional exhaustion from the recent events.

Phoebe stood on the deck of her cottage... now their cottage, watching the sunset paint the bay in golden hues. Strong arms wrapped around her waist as Leon pressed against her back.

"Happy?" he murmured into her neck.

"Mmm. The resort's running better than ever, Sophie's settled in perfectly..." She turned in his arms. "And I'm madly in love with my boss."

"Ex-boss," he corrected. "You run this place now. Though I do enjoy when you call me 'boss' in bed."

Phoebe laughed, then grew thoughtful watching Sophie walking along the beach below with another figure, their animated conversation carrying faintly on the breeze. Sophie seemed more relaxed than she had in years.

"She seems to be finding her place here," Leon observed.

"Yeah..." Phoebe smiled. "Everything's working out better than I could have imagined."

"Speaking of working out..." Leon's hands slid down to

cup her ass. "I believe we have some celebrating to do. Lynn's retirement party was perfect."

"That's because I'm amazing at my job," she purred, grinding against the growing bulge in his shorts.

"You're amazing at everything." He scooped her up, carrying her inside. "And I plan to spend the rest of my life showing you just how much I appreciate that."

As their bedroom door closed, distant laughter drifted up from the beach where the last rays of sun painted the peaceful scene in shades of possibility.

more from me

All of my books are available on my website. Join my newsletter for exclusive free goodies and updates!

Visit JessieCooke.com

Printed in Great Britain
by Amazon